OUR PRAIRIE HOME
A Picture Album

Every time Alvina finds Long John Silver asleep on her bed, she tells him, "Come on. Shake a leg!"

OUR PRAIRIE HOME
A Picture Album

BROOKE GOFFSTEIN

HARPER & ROW, PUBLISHERS

Our Prairie Home
Copyright © 1988 by Brooke Goffstein
Printed in the U.S.A. All rights reserved.
Typography by Al Cetta

Library of Congress Cataloging-in-Publication Data
Goffstein, M. B.
    Our prairie home: a picture album/Brooke Goffstein.—1st ed.
        p.   cm.
    "A Charlotte Zolotow book."
    Summary: A day goes by in the life of a family of 2-inch-tall
wooden figures in their prairie home.
    ISBN 0-06-022290-5: $
    ISBN 0-06-022291-3 (lib. bdg.): $
    [1. Family life—Fiction.   2. Dolls—Fiction.]   I. Title.
PZ7.G55730p 1988   87-30795
[E]—dc19   CIP
                                                        AC

1 2 3 4 5 6 7 8 9 10
First Edition

Paintings *Pink Robe, Blue Gown,* and *Long John,* and Alvina's pink dress, by Kate Spohn. Stovepipe by Brian Woods. Window screen courtesy of Constance Fogler. Walls and floor courtesy of Raimundo Lemus. Ceiling courtesy of Bob Goffstein. Hello to Iris Brown and Ken Hansen. Thanks always to C.Z., John Vitale, Abby Sundell, Antonia Markiet, Alan Horowitz, and Constance Fogler.

ALVINA listens to the radio, hoping to hear one of the jokes she sent in to her favorite show.

Her sister, Lillian, washes the dinner dishes.

Lillian's husband, Bernard, is out on the porch with the cat, Long John Silver.

Ten-year-old Mildred looks at herself in the mirror in Alvina's room, and hopes she will be like her Aunt Alvina.

Within the first half hour of Alvina's coming to live with them, Mildred brought in her doll Inez, and Alvina exclaimed, "Oh, for cute!"

Once, when Alvina dropped a dish, she said, "Oh, for crying in the beer!"

One time, when Alvina was changing clothes, she said to Mildred, "Don't mind my bare back!"

Sometimes Lillian is as grouchy as a bear to Alvina.

Lillian isn't used to having someone at home with her all day long.

She likes to take a nap in the afternoon.

She wants Alvina to get a job, so she reminds Alvina that she taught grade school before she married Bernard.

Since Alvina had to stay on the farm because Lillian went to Teachers College, she says, "Go kiss a fly!"

Alvina laughs so hard at her own wit that Lillian tells her, "Laughing makes you fat."

Long John Silver takes a sip of milk.

Mother and Aunt hear Mildred's step on the porch.

It was Instrument Day at Mildred's school, and
she brings home a French horn. She has signed up
for lessons.